Diaries

D0062225

Look for more

TWO of a kind ™

titles:

TWO of a kind™
Diaries
Santa Girls

by Diana G. Gallagher
from the series created by
Robert Griffard & Howard Adler

HarperEntertainment
An Imprint of **HarperCollins***Publishers*

A PARACHUTE PRESS BOOK

A PARACHUTE PRESS BOOK

Parachute Publishing, L.L.C.
156 Fifth Avenue
Suite 302
New York, NY 10010

Published by
HarperEntertainment
An Imprint of HarperCollins*Publishers*
10 East 53rd Street, New York, NY 10022-5299

TWO OF A KIND books created and produced by Parachute Press, L.L.C., in cooperation with Dualstar Publications, a division of Dualstar Entertainment Group, LLC, published by HarperEntertainment, an imprint of HarperCollins Publishers.

ISBN 0-06-009328-5

HarperCollins®, ®, and HarperEntertainment™ are trademarks of HarperCollins Publishers Inc.

First printing: December 2003

Printed in the United States of America

Visit HarperEntertainment on the World Wide Web at
www.harpercollins.com

10 9 8 7 6 5 4 3 2 1

Friday

Dear Diary,

I can't believe it's only two weeks until Christmas vacation! I've been so busy Christmas shopping, I haven't had time to write in days.

I have a secret, and I just *know* I'm going to talk! I'm so bad at keeping good stuff to myself. But this is a supersecret. I can't let my twin sister, Ashley, find out that I got her the one thing she really wants for Christmas.

 I'm sitting on my bed looking out the window. It's snowing here at White Oak Academy in New Hampshire. The campus looks like a beautiful winter wonderland.

The whole school is excited about the holidays. At lunch today no one could talk about anything else. All my friends are into cool holiday projects.

Elise van Hook loves anything that glitters, so she's in charge of the Porter House decorating committee.

"We're putting up the tree tomorrow," Elise said. Her Christmas charm bracelet jingled when she

1

moved her arm. "When we're done, the lounge will look better than the mall!"

Phoebe Cahill, Ashley's roommate, frowned. "I hope the committee isn't going to do anything weird to the tree. I like old-fashioned, real, green Christmas trees with colored balls and candy canes and tinsel."

"Don't worry, Phoebe. Our tree will be traditional," Elise said.

"With colored lights?" Cheryl Miller looked up.

"Colored lights aren't traditional," Elise said. "Besides, they'd clash with the red bows and candy canes. We're using all white lights."

I didn't say anything, but I really like colored lights. Ashley is a white-light person. We've got an every-other-year plan at our house that keeps everyone happy half the time.

Cheryl brightened. "I bet the Senior Center will have blinking colored lights on their tree."

"How are the rehearsals going?" I asked. The First Form Chorus was giving a Christmas concert at the Senior Center. At White Oak Academy, they call the seventh grade "First Form."

"Not all that great," Cheryl said. "I'm supposed to sing harmony, but I keep singing the melody by mistake."

"Harmony is hard," Summer Sorenson said.

"I'm fine when I sing with Ms. O'Neal's rehearsal

tape," Cheryl explained. "I just hit the wrong notes when I sing with other people."

"I'll help you practice, Cheryl," I said. "I'm not a great singer but I can carry a tune. At least well enough to help you learn your harmonies."

I had plenty of time to help because this year I had done my Christmas shopping early. But I was so busy shopping, I'd forgotten to sign up for a project.

"Thanks, Mary-Kate." Cheryl looked relieved.

"Who wants to go to the mall on Sunday?" Summer asked.

"Me!" Ashley said. "I haven't gotten any gifts for anyone yet."

"I just love the mall this time of year," Summer said. "Back home in California, the mall is the only place that *looks* like Christmas, because it's always warm and sunny outside."

"Christmas in California must be fun," Phoebe said. "When you finish your shopping, you can hit the beach."

"Exactly," Summer said, giggling.

"Don't you have shopping to do, Mary-Kate?" Ashley asked. She picked up a french fry and popped it into her mouth.

"Except for friends, all my shopping is done," I said.

"Even for me?" Ashley teased.

I clamped my lips shut. I was not going to spoil Ashley's surprise.

"Maybe we shouldn't give gifts to one another. We should only buy a present for our roommate," Elise said. "I barely have enough money to buy presents for my family."

"That's cool with me," Ashley said. "I'm hoping I can find things on sale. That's the only way I'll be able to buy gifts for everyone on my list."

That's what I did. I saved money last summer, and I had the extra money our dad sent for Christmas presents. I bought things on sale right after Thanksgiving.

"I vote for no friend gifts, too." Cheryl pushed her tray aside and folded her arms on the table. "I want to spend my money on something extra nice for my parents this year."

"So we're all agreed? No gifts." Elise looked around the table and everyone nodded.

"Just don't forget the Headmistress Gift Fund," Campbell reminded us. She was in charge of collecting a dollar from each of the First Form students.

"What did the committee decide to get Mrs. Pritchard?" Summer asked.

4

"Nothing yet," Campbell said. "Any ideas?"

"I saw these dynamite ice skates at Sports Mania," I joked.

Phoebe raised an eyebrow. "I don't think Mrs. Pritchard wants ice skates."

"But Mary-Kate does, right?" Ashley grinned.

"Well, yeah," I admitted. Ashley and I like different things, but she knows me better than anyone. "I'm hoping Great-aunt Morgan sends us Christmas checks again this year so I can buy them."

"I hope she does, too." Ashley crossed her fingers on both hands. "That jacket we saw at Teen Town last month is the *only* thing I really want this year."

I pretended I didn't remember. "The black one with the leather trim, the fitted waist, and the tie belt?"

"That's the one." Ashley glanced at her watch and jumped up. "Uh-oh. I promised Mrs. Yancosek I'd return an overdue library book by yesterday, and I keep forgetting!"

"Mrs. Yancosek is usually pretty understanding." Elise sipped the last of her milk and crumpled the container.

"This book was due a month ago." Ashley shrugged as the bell rang. "I guess one more day won't matter."

I held my breath as Ashley hurried out of the dining hall with Elise, Cheryl, Phoebe, and Summer. Then I exhaled and slumped in my chair.

"What's the matter, Mary-Kate?" Campbell asked. Campbell and I have been best friends since my first day at White Oak. She knows me almost as well as Ashley does.

"Keeping-a-secret-itis." I was only half-joking.

"From me?" Campbell asked as we headed to our classes.

"From Ashley," I confessed. I could trust Campbell not to tell. "I got her that jacket for Christmas."

"Wow!" Campbell exclaimed. "Ashley's been talking about that jacket for weeks. She is going to be so surprised!"

"If I don't blab before Christmas and spoil it," I said.

I suddenly realized I was more excited about giving Ashley her jacket than I was about getting presents.

And that, Diary, just made waiting worse.

Dear Diary,

What a day! I'm in bed now, wearing my new Christmas pajamas. It's almost time for lights-out, so I'll write fast.

You won't believe this, Diary, but Mary-Kate

called me on the phone and asked me for advice on what to wear! I was so shocked, I hung up without asking *why* her outfit was important. Or where she was going or when or anything.

Mary-Kate is usually more worried about sports scores than clothes. *That* should have been my first clue! But I didn't even suspect my sneaky sister was up to something.

I hurried down the stairs to the dorm room she shares with Campbell. I found Mary-Kate folding laundry.

"So what's the big fashion emergency?" I asked.

"Christmas," Mary-Kate said. She kept folding laundry. She didn't look at me.

That was the second clue. *What's she hiding?* I wondered. Mary-Kate is the absolute *worst* at keeping secrets. That's because her face always gives her away!

Mary-Kate pulled a big box out from under the pile of clothes. "I wanted to give you this."

"What is it?" I asked. TEEN TOWN was written in gold on the green gift box. A stretchy gold ribbon and bow held the box closed. *Clothes!* I thought.

"It's cold and snowing, and, well—" Mary-Kate shrugged.

"I just thought it was silly to wait until Christmas to give you something you can use now."

"You're giving me my Christmas present *now*?" I sat on the edge of Campbell's bed. "But I don't have yours yet."

"That's okay," Mary-Kate said. "Open it."

"Okay." I slipped the ribbon off the box and lifted the lid. When I unfolded the tissue paper, I just stared. Mary-Kate had gotten me the black jacket with the leather trim I wanted so much!

"Well?" Mary-Kate said.

"I can't believe it!" I squealed. "This is so cool!"

Mary-Kate just grinned.

Campbell came in as I slipped on the jacket and tied the belt. She paused in the doorway, shaking her head.

"Well, so much for that surprise," Campbell said.

"Believe me, Campbell," Mary-Kate said. "Ashley was *totally* surprised."

"Flabbergasted!" I added. That's our dad's favorite word when he's really surprised.

"I knew you'd break, Mary-Kate," Campbell teased.

"I wanted to see the look on Ashley's face when she opened the box," Mary-Kate explained. "Even if it is two weeks early."

This time I was thrilled that Mary-Kate couldn't

keep a secret! "It fits perfectly," I said. "I totally love it, Mary-Kate. I just love it!" I gave my sister a huge hug.

"Are you still coming to help me collect for Mrs. Pritchard's gift?" Campbell looked at Mary-Kate.

Mary-Kate hesitated.

"Go on, Mary-Kate," I said. "I want to show my new jacket to Phoebe. And anyone else I can find!"

I was so excited, I didn't take the jacket off. I ran up the stairs to my room on the third floor. I saw Elise in the hall and twirled to show off the jacket.

"It's my Christmas present from Mary-Kate!"

"That is so cool!" Elise said. "Looks like we both had a lucky day. I just got this fabulous skirt from my mom."

Elise held up a red suede skirt with green suede holly leaves stitched on the side pockets.

"It's gorgeous!" I said.

I ran down the hall to my room. Phoebe wasn't there, but I'd show her my new jacket later. I had something else to do.

Mary-Kate and I always buy each other nice Christmas gifts, but Mary-Kate has never bought anything as fabulous as the jacket.

No wonder she can't buy the ice skates she wants, I thought. *Mary-Kate spent most of her Christmas money on me!*

I knew the jacket cost about fifty dollars. I absolutely had to do something just as thoughtful for my sister. She really wanted those Olympic Gold ice skates. But I was sure Mary-Kate would buy them as soon as Great-aunt Morgan's check arrived. Great-aunt Morgan sends each of us fifty dollars every year.

I had to think of something else.

While I waited for Phoebe to get back, I made a list with three columns.

In the first column, I wrote down the names of everyone I had to buy gifts for. My dad, Phoebe, my boyfriend, Ross Lambert, Great-aunt Morgan, and Mary-Kate were all on my list.

The next column was *Gift Idea.* I left that one blank. The third column was *Cost.* Blank, too. Time to check my money.

I pulled out my wallet and counted the money inside. I only had twenty-five dollars. Yikes! Where had all my money gone?

My dad had sent us each seventy-five dollars at Thanksgiving. That was three weeks ago. I had gone to a movie and bought my favorite fashion magazines. I also bought sodas and a new paperback mystery novel.

I looked at the page in my notebook where I wrote down what I spent. When I added everything up, it came to twenty-eight dollars. Where was the missing thirty-two dollars?

Then I remembered that last week I bought Christmas flannel pj's and a matching robe for myself. New Hampshire winter nights are really cold. The funky red flannel pj's are toasty warm. But now I only had enough money to spend five dollars on each person on my list!

I couldn't get Mary-Kate anything cool for five dollars! I thought about calling Dad to ask for more money. Not a good idea. He's always lecturing me about how much money I spend shopping.

I looked around my room. I didn't have anything to sell that anyone would want to buy!

My only hope is that Great-aunt Morgan's check gets here soon.

I'm going to spend the whole fifty dollars on a great present for my sister!

Chapter 2

Saturday

Dear Diary,

I'm usually excited when I get a package slip in my mailbox. Ashley and I have aunts who send cookies  and friends who send CDs and magazines. Boxes always have good things in them.

So that's why I was so confused, Diary. Today I got a box from Great-aunt Morgan. She *always* sends our Christmas check in an envelope. Did she send cookies *and* a check this year? Or maybe presents and a check? Why did she send a box?

The box was addressed to me and Ashley. I almost ripped it open, but then I remembered that Ashley and I have a deal. If a box has both our names on it, we open it together.

I ran up the stairs to Ashley's room and opened the door without knocking. Ashley was at her desk doing homework.

"Look what we got." I held up the box. "It's from Great-aunt Morgan."

"Great-aunt Morgan?" Ashley frowned. "She's never sent our Christmas checks in a box before."

12

"I know." I didn't want to sound greedy, but Great-aunt Morgan's money was my only hope of getting new ice skates.

"I wonder what's in it," Ashley said. "Should we wait until Christmas or open it now?"

"I vote for now," I said.

"Me, too." Ashley ripped the tape off the box and lifted the flaps. There were two gift boxes inside. The green one had my name on it, the red had Ashley's.

Not skates, I thought when Ashley handed the green box to me. It was too light. *Probably clothes.*

Ashley loves getting new clothes, even for Christmas, but she looked disappointed, too. Still, she did a great job of pretending to be thrilled when she opened the red box.

"Red mittens!" Ashley exclaimed. "Just what I needed. There's a hole in my old ones." She read the attached tag. "Great-aunt Morgan knitted these herself. Isn't that cool?"

I had to admit it was pretty cool. Great-aunt Morgan is over seventy years old. She doesn't see very well, and her fingers get stiff with arthritis. It must have taken her a long time to knit Ashley's mittens.

"What did you get?" Ashley pointed to my box.

Great-aunt Morgan *is* our favorite aunt. I made

up my mind to like whatever she had sent me.

"Let's see." I opened the box and gasped.

Ashley leaned forward. "What?"

"This." I held up my present. The  hand-knit black vest had three big yellow buttons and yellow and green pom-poms around the bottom.

"Oh." Ashley's eyes widened. "That's . . . that's the ugliest vest I've ever seen."

"Yeah, it sure is." I slowly sat down on Ashley's bed. "I really wanted money to buy skates."

"I know." Ashley sat down beside me. "Still, there is one good thing about that vest."

"No, there's not." I wasn't in the mood to be teased. The vest was ugly. Really ugly.

"Yes, there is," Ashley said. "Great-aunt Morgan doesn't visit, so you'll *never* have to wear it!"

"I hadn't thought of that," I said.

Ashley had a good point. If Great-aunt Morgan came to see us at White Oak, I'd *have* to wear that awful vest! There was no way Ashley or I would *ever* hurt Great-aunt Morgan's feelings. Luckily, that wasn't a problem.

"Except for now." Ashley opened her drawer.

"No way!" I exclaimed. "I'm not wearing this vest."

"Just this once." Ashley held up a camera. "We have to send Great-aunt Morgan a picture so she knows we got the box."

"Great idea!" I meant it.

I took Ashley's picture first. The red mittens actually looked good with the black leather jacket. I put on the vest. Ugh! The yellow and green pompoms looked terrible with my red and gray rugby shirt. Ashley loaned me a white shirt for the photo. Better——but the vest was still ugly.

"Smile!" Ashley raised the camera.

I struck a model's pose with my head thrown back a little. Then Ashley burst out laughing.

"This isn't funny, Ashley."

"I'm sorry, Mary-Kate." Ashley giggled. "But that vest is hilarious!"

I glanced down at the yellow and green pompoms. I didn't feel like laughing, but I couldn't help it.

The hideous black vest *was* funny!

Dear Diary,

Great-aunt Morgan's package solved one of my problems. Since she sent Mary-Kate the vest, Mary-Kate won't be able to buy ice skates. So I don't have to worry about *what* to get Mary-Kate. Now I just have to worry about how to pay for it.

I thought about taking my Christmas robe and pj's back to the store and getting my money back. But I've been wearing them for a week!

Today after classes I went to the mall with Summer. I didn't have much money, but I wanted to window-shop for ideas.

Summer grinned as we entered the mall. "Wow! It looks just like Christmas in here."

"It feels like Christmas, too," I said. There's something special about malls at Christmastime. The glittering decorations and holiday music cheered me up.

There just has to be a way to get those ice skates for Mary-Kate! I thought.

We walked toward the far end of the mall.

"Hey!" Summer pointed at the bookstore window display. "Phoebe might like that book of old movie posters."

I had told Summer who was on my Christmas list. But I didn't tell her that I didn't have much money. The book was probably too expensive, but I went inside to check.

"How much is the movie-poster book in the window?" I asked the clerk behind the counter.

"It's on sale for fifteen dollars," the clerk said.

"Thanks." I looked through the book. It had all the posters from Phoebe's favorite old movies.

I put the book back and pulled my list out of my backpack. Next to Phoebe's name I wrote the gift. Then I wrote the price in the cost column.

"I thought we decided not to exchange gifts with friends," Summer said as we left the bookstore.

"Except for roommates," I said. Phoebe is almost as close as my sister. "I *have* to get Phoebe something nice."

Summer nodded. "Who's next?"

We went to the luggage store to find a gift for my dad. I've been giving him cologne every year since I was four. This year I wanted to do something different.

"Boy, could my dad use one of these!" I pointed to a zippered notebook with plastic pockets instead of pages. The pockets had double seals.

"He's traveling, right?" Summer asked.

"He's doing research in the Amazon," I said. "It rains a lot there. This will keep all his important papers dry."

"Then it's the perfect gift," Summer said.

Not exactly, I thought. The notebook came in two sizes. The smaller one cost twenty-five dollars. The larger one cost thirty-five. Even the smaller notebook would take all the money I had.

I wrote the notebook and prices on my list anyway. *Maybe someone else will send me Christmas money*

17

I can spend on gifts. If not, I thought, *I can always buy Dad cologne again.* "Lets go to Sports Mania next," I said. "I want to find out how much ice skates cost."

"For Mary-Kate?" Summer looked impressed. "You are so sweet. Everyone knows how much Mary-Kate wants those skates."

"But I may not have enough money to get them. So don't say anything, okay?"

"Not a word." Summer made a lips-zipped gesture.

Sports Mania had a few pairs of Olympic Gold ice skates in Mary-Kate's size. They cost forty dollars!

"Yikes!" Summer said. "Forty dollars is a lot of money."

Especially when I have five people on my list and only twenty-five dollars to spend! I thought.

A saleswoman by the cash register heard us. "A week from Thursday those skates will be on sale for thirty dollars."

"Thirty dollars?" I repeated to be sure.

The saleswoman nodded. "But I can't promise that we'll still have them in your size."

"Thanks, anyway," I said. Thirty dollars wasn't a great deal and it was more than I had. There was no way—even on sale—that I could get Mary-Kate those skates.

"I'm hungry," Summer said. "Let's get a snack at the Cookie Cutter."

I left the store feeling worse than when I went in. The white skates had gleaming silver blades and a small picture of an Olympic torch on the white leather boots. It just wasn't fair that I couldn't give Mary-Kate the one  thing she really wanted for Christmas.

If there really is a Santa Claus, I'll get the money somewhere, I told myself.

Okay, so that was a totally silly thought. But Christmas was coming, and I was desperate!

Summer and I reached the center of the mall. The usual benches and potted trees had been moved to make room for Santa's Station.

"Wow!" Summer stared in awe.

I stared, too.

Several Christmas trees towered over the North Pole setting. They were covered in fake snow with white lights, gold bows, and red ornaments. Plastic reindeer, elves, and giant candy canes stood on mounds of cotton around a red sleigh. The sleigh was piled with presents.

Santa Claus sat on a golden throne. Mrs. Claus

stepped out of a small building that had been decorated to
look like a gingerbread house.

The Santa scene was fan-
tastic, but that's not what had
caught my eye. I stared at a
sign by the rope gate.

SANTA GIRL WANTED

Maybe Santa Claus is coming to my rescue! I
thought. I didn't know exactly what a Santa Girl
was, but it didn't really matter. If Santa was paying
money, this was the job for me.

"My stomach is rumbling for warm oatmeal-
raisin cookies," Summer said. "Let's go!"

"You go on," I said. "I'll meet you in a minute."

I was afraid to tell Summer that I was going to
try to be a Santa Girl. I had never applied for a job
before. If Santa turned me down, I didn't want my
friend to see.

Mrs. Claus had rosy cheeks and curly white hair.
She wore a candy-striped blouse and a ruffled white
apron. She was taking a picture of a little boy on
Santa's lap.

I took a deep breath and walked over to her.

Mrs. Claus smiled at me. "Can I help you?"

I was so nervous. "I want the Santa Girl job," I blurted out.

"Oh, my," Mrs. Claus said. "How old are you?"

"Twelve," I said. "But I'm a really good worker."

"That's younger than I wanted," Mrs. Claus said.

My heart sank. No job, no money, no skates for Mary-Kate. I had to win Mrs. Claus over. "I can work every afternoon and weekends, too."

"Do you have baby-sitting experience?" Mrs. Claus asked.

"Not much," I answered truthfully. "Why?"

"We need someone to help keep the children happy." Mrs. Claus had a kind smile. "They get restless if they have to wait in line too long."

"Excuse me!" A woman at the far end of the counter waved. "Are my photographs ready?"

"Stay here," Mrs. Claus said to me. "I'll be back."

I started to feel hopeful. Mrs. Claus had not asked me to leave. *Is she just being polite?* I wondered. *Or do I maybe have a chance of getting this job?*

Chapter 3

Sunday

Dear Diary,

An older girl stood by the rope gate. She had short dark hair, blue eyes, and freckles. She wore a green vest over a white blouse, a red skirt, white tights with pointed green shoes, and a red Santa cap. Her nametag read: SHELLY. She had to be a Santa Girl.

"Are you ready to see Santa?" the Santa Girl asked the next kid in line.

"No!" The little girl ducked behind her mother.

"Don't be afraid, Mandy," the girl's mother said. "Santa is the one who brings toys to children on Christmas Eve."

"He'll give you a candy cane right now," Shelly added with a smile. "Come on, Mandy. I'll take you to see Santa."

Shelly led Mandy to the throne while Mandy's mother ordered a photo from Mrs. Claus.

I watched Shelly while I waited. I could tell she was an excellent helper. When Santa patted his knee, Shelly waited until Mandy nodded. Then she lifted the little girl up.

"You're next, Ronald," a woman in line said to her son.

"I don't want to!" Ronald clung to his mother's hand. Tears streamed down his cheeks.

"You know what, Ronald?" I said. "When I was little I was afraid of Santa, too. Now he's one of my best friends."

"He is?" Ronald looked up at me.

"Absolutely!" I leaned over and whispered, "Santa brings me all kinds of cool stuff every Christmas."

Ronald looked doubtful. "Will he bring me presents?"

"Of course! That's what Santa does," I said. "But first you have to tell him what you want."

Shelly came back to get Ronald. Ronald scrambled right up onto Santa's lap.

Mrs. Claus smiled and waved for me to come over to the counter. "You handled that very well, Miss—"

"Ashley Burke," I said.

"Well, Ashley, if you want to be a Santa Girl, you're hired. You can start Tuesday afternoon."

"I can?" I squealed with joy. "This is so great!"

"Be here at ten minutes to four," Mrs. Claus said.

"We have a Santa Girl costume that will fit you perfectly!"

"I'll be here," I said.

I wanted to jump up and down with excitement. Now I could buy Mary-Kate's skates. *And I get to wear that cute outfit*, I thought.

I turned. Dana Woletsky was staring at me. Dana is the snobbiest girl in First Form at White Oak.

"Did you just get a job, Ashley?" Dana asked, frowning.

"Yes, I did." I didn't mean to sound smug, but I couldn't help it. Dana is always giving me and Mary-Kate a hard time about something.

"Well, you'd better quit now," Dana said. "Mrs. Pritchard has a strict rule about students working. They can't."

"Oh, no!" I moaned. I had forgotten about the no job rule! Mrs. Pritchard never lets students work during school. She says it takes away from our studies.

Somehow, Diary, I have to convince Mrs. Pritchard to let me be a Santa Girl. I just have to!

Dear Diary,

For someone who didn't sign up for a special Christmas project, I sure was busy today. This morning I met Cheryl in the music room.

"I need help!" she said. "The Senior Center Christmas Concert is this Sunday. I don't have much time to learn the songs."

Ms. O'Neal had recorded the melody and harmony parts separately. Cheryl played the tape of the alto section singing "Winter Wonderland." Then she sang the harmony perfectly.

"You didn't miss a note," I said.

Cheryl shrugged. "That's because I was singing alone."

"Let's try it together."

I sang the melody. But Cheryl sang so softly, I couldn't tell if she sang the harmony okay or not. I thought about it for a moment. I was pretty sure Cheryl knew her part. She just needed a confidence boost.

"Wow! You really have a great voice," I said.

"You really think so?" Cheryl asked uncertainly.

"Absolutely," I told her. "Try singing harmony with the melody tape."

Cheryl turned on the player and started singing softly.

I smiled to encourage her, and it worked! By the end of the song, she was singing perfect harmony. We practiced until lunchtime and I promised Cheryl that we'd practice again later this week. Then I looked for Summer.

All afternoon I helped Summer make table decorations for the First Form holiday party.

Then I went to admire the Porter House Christmas tree with Elise. It looked fantastic. The tree was covered with white lights, candy canes, silver and gold balls, and red bows.

After dinner I helped Campbell collect for Mrs. Pritchard's gift. Campbell is at a Gift Committee meeting now. I'm tired, but helping everyone has really made me feel like Christmas—

Sorry, but I had to leave, Diary. Summer just came by.

"What's up?" I asked. "Did we forget to make something for the party?"

Summer shook her head. "No. Thanks to you, everything's done. That's why I'm here. To thank you with this." Summer pulled a gift box out from behind her back.

"But—" I was so surprised, I just stood there.

Summer rushed to explain. "I know we decided not to exchange gifts, but Ashley said that roommates didn't count."

Now I was really confused. Summer wasn't my roommate.

"So a friend who helped me make party decorations all afternoon doesn't count, either." Summer shoved the box at me.

"Open it," she said.

I opened it. "This is so cool! A Chicago Cubs baseball jersey! How did you know they're my favorite team?"

"Maybe because you're from Chicago?" Summer grinned. "I saw it at the mall today, and I just had to get it for you."

I panicked. I had nothing for her. I know Summer didn't expect a gift in return, but I felt bad not giving her anything. Then I saw the gift box from Great-aunt Morgan on my desk. Brainstorm!

I gave Summer the box. "I didn't have time to wrap it."

"Wow! What a surprise!" Summer smiled when she saw the black vest. "Is this handmade?" she asked.

"It's the only one like it in the whole world."

I never thought *anyone* would want that awful vest, but Summer likes unusual stuff. She seemed really happy.

And Great-aunt Morgan will never know.

Chapter 4

Monday

Dear Diary,

I went to Mrs. Pritchard's office first thing this morning. I knew the headmistress *never* gives anyone permission to take a job. But I couldn't get Mary-Kate's ice skates without one!

Mrs. Pritchard frowned when I explained. "White Oak students aren't allowed to work, Ashley," she said.

"It's not a permanent job, Mrs. Pritchard."

Mrs. Pritchard sighed. "School must come first."

"The other Santa Girl is in school, too," I said. I didn't mention that Shelly was in high school. "Can't you *please* make an exception this one time?"

Mrs. Pritchard shook her head.

I couldn't give up without a fight. "I don't have any tests before vacation, and all my papers are done," I said. "And I won't miss any classes because I'll be working after school."

Mrs. Pritchard didn't look convinced.

"Christmas is about giving, Mrs. Pritchard," I argued. "Without a job, I'll have to ask my dad for more money. But I want to *earn* the money myself. Then giving presents will really mean something."

Mrs. Pritchard nodded.

Was that a good sign? I kept talking. "Santa Girls are just like baby-sitters, except the parents are right there!"

Mrs. Pritchard sighed again. "Okay—"

"Okay?" I inhaled sharply. "I can have the job?"

"That's not what I meant." Mrs. Pritchard peered at me over her rhinestone glasses. "But I'll think about it. See me at the end of classes today."

I left the office with my fingers crossed. At least Mrs. Pritchard hadn't said no.

Dear Diary,

After class today I sat on the floor in my room surrounded by paper, bows,

and tags. I'm not very good at wrapping presents, but I love doing it anyway. Getting ready for Christmas is almost as much fun as Christmas Day.

When the phone rang, I expected it to be Ashley. She was waiting for Mrs. Pritchard to tell her whether she could be a Santa's helper at the mall. Personally, *nothing* could get me to wear a costume with green elf shoes and white tights!

But it wasn't Ashley. It was Great-aunt Morgan.

"What a surprise, Aunt Morgan!" We call her Aunt Morgan for short when we're talking to her. "Your package came."

"Did you open it?" Great-aunt Morgan asked.

"Yes," I admitted. "We were so excited, we couldn't wait. Ashley loves the red mittens. She needed new ones."

"I'm delighted to hear that!" Great-aunt Morgan sounded pleased. "Does the vest fit you all right?"

"It's a perfect fit!" *That's the truth*, I thought. "You knitted it, right?"

"Yes, I did. I designed it, too," Great-aunt Morgan said proudly.

"It's very . . . unusual," I said. "Ashley and I took pictures of us wearing our gifts to send you."

"That was thoughtful but not necessary," Great-aunt Morgan said. "You and Ashley can wear them when I take you out to lunch a week from Friday."

"Lunch?" I tried not to sound shocked. "Where?"

"Wherever you girls want to go," Great aunt Morgan said. "I'll pick you up at White Oak at noon."

"But I thought you didn't travel anymore," I sputtered.

"Oh, I don't usually," Great-aunt Morgan said. "But I'm spending Christmas with Uncle Sid in Maine. I'll pass right by White Oak on my way."

But I don't have the vest! I thought in a panic.

30

"It's a long way from Boston to Maine, Aunt Morgan," I said. "Should you be driving so far by yourself?"

It's not that I didn't want to see her. I did. In the summer—when it's too hot to wear a knit vest!

Great-aunt Morgan laughed. "I'm old, but I can still get around."

"Great." I felt numb when I hung up. Great-aunt Morgan would be crushed when she found out I gave her gift away.

I had to get the ugly vest back from Summer—quick!

Dear Diary,

I was nervous as I walked toward Mrs. Pritchard's office. I would find out if I could be a Santa Girl or not.

Please, don't let it be not!

I knocked on Mrs. Pritchard's door.

"Come in." Mrs. Pritchard smiled when I stepped inside. "You really want this job, don't you?"

"Yes, Mrs. Pritchard," I said. "I really do."

"Good. Because Mrs. Amberly expects you to be on time tomorrow," Mrs. Pritchard said.

"Mrs. Amberly?" I frowned. Who was Mrs. Amberly?

Mrs. Pritchard grinned. "Mr. Amberly is the

Santa Claus at the mall every year. He and Mrs. Amberly prefer to be called Santa and Mrs. Claus in December."

"On time?" I suddenly realized what Mrs. Pritchard just said. I couldn't be late for work! "I can have the job?"

Mrs. Pritchard nodded. "Santa and his wife are respected members of the community. I called and talked to them. The job pays five dollars an hour. It's only two hours a day for ten days, until their usual Santa Girl gets home from college."

That was one day before Mary-Kate and I went home for Christmas vacation.

"Thank you so much!" It took all of my willpower to walk out of the office without whooping for joy. When I was halfway down the hall, I stopped to give myself a two-fisted *Yes!* Then I raced to Porter House to drop off my books.

I dashed into my room and calculated my pay. Two hours a day for ten days equaled one hundred dollars.

I went over my list of the presents I wanted to buy. The waterproof notebook for Dad was twenty-five dollars, the movie poster book for Phoebe was fifteen, and Mary-Kate's skates on sale would be thirty. That was seventy dollars. Plus I wanted to get two other presents. I'd need twenty-five dollars for Ross's History Trivia Cards, and thirty dollars for Great-aunt Morgan's electric throw blanket—it all came to one hundred and twenty-five dollars!

Exactly what I'll have with my Santa Girl pay and the money left over from Dad! I realized.

Campbell came into our room then. "I need to collect your dollar for the Headmistress Gift Fund."

I had forgotten about the gift for Mrs. Pritchard. And I *really* owed her this year for letting me be a Santa Girl!

I found a dollar in change in my desk and gave it to Campbell. That dollar wouldn't make a difference, but I couldn't afford any more money surprises.

I was going to make just enough money being a Santa Girl to buy my Christmas presents. I couldn't spend one extra penny on anything else.

That was going to take a lot more willpower than I usually had!

Chapter 5

Tuesday

Dear Diary,

I didn't want everyone to know I had re-gifted Great-aunt Morgan's vest to Summer or that I needed it back! So I spent most of today trying to get Summer alone.

My chance came when she was practicing basketball with Lexy Martin. They were signed up to play in a charity game between White Oak and a local school next Saturday.

"Perfect timing!" Summer said when I walked into the gym. "We need you to be on the team."

"Desperately," Lexy added. She held the basketball under her arm. "Karen Reedy had to drop out, and you're a great player, Mary-Kate."

"We're raising money for a toy giveaway," Summer said.

"Please, Mary-Kate." Lexy clasped her hands. "All you have to do is find a few people who will pay a dollar for every point you make."

"I have six pledges," Summer said. "The problem is, usually I don't make many baskets."

"But you'll be trying, Summer,

and that's the important part," Lexy said. "It doesn't even matter who wins the game! People pay for *every* point that's scored."

"Sounds like fun," I said. "Count me in."

The game was just four days away. That wasn't much time to find people to pay for my points.

"Excellent!" Lexy turned and dribbled down the court.

I finally had a few minutes alone with Summer.

"I don't know how to say this except to just say it." I exhaled. "My Great-aunt Morgan gave me that vest, Summer, and I re-gifted it to you. I wanted to give you something because you gave me the Cubs jersey, and the vest was all I had."

"Oh, well—" Summer sighed.

Passing on unwanted gifts is an awful thing to do to a friend. I felt like a jerk for dumping the vest on Summer.

"I'll get you something else, Summer," I promised. "Something really nice that's especially for you."

"You don't have to do that, Mary-Kate," Summer said.

"Yes, I do." I couldn't look her in the eye, so I stared at my feet. "Because I need to get the vest back."

"What?" Summer looked confused.

"It's really important, Summer, or I wouldn't ask." I sounded desperate because I was desperate. "My Great-aunt Morgan is coming to see me, and I *have* to wear that vest."

Summer winced. "I, uh—gave it to Dana."

My heart skipped a beat. "You gave my gift away? To Dana Woletsky?"

"Yeah." Summer nodded.

I groaned and slumped against the wall. Anybody but Dana!

Dana Woletsky loves to make my life difficult.

Getting my vest back from her was not going to be easy!

Dear Diary,

The first day at work is the same as the first day at a new school. You're excited and scared because you don't know what to expect. Parts of being a Santa Girl were just as great as I imagined. Other parts were definitely not!

Shelly, the other Santa Girl, is Mrs. Claus and Santa's niece. She's sixteen and thinks the red and green colors in the Santa Girl costume clash with her blue eyes.

I noticed a gorgeous blue sweater with a matching knit hat on the chair with Shelly's street clothes:

blue jeans and a white shirt. Obviously, Shelly's favorite color is blue.

"I can't believe my aunt found someone small enough to wear Natalie's outfit," Shelly said.

"Natalie is your older sister, right?" I pinned my nametag on the green vest. I thought the costume was adorable. Wearing it made me *feel* like a Christmas elf.

"Yes, but she went to college last fall," Shelly said. "She doesn't get home for vacation until late next week. That's why we needed you."

"Let's go, girls!" Mrs. Claus called.

"Don't worry, Ashley." Shelly gave me an encouraging smile. "If you like kids and have truckloads of patience, this job is a snap."

"You must like it," I said. Mrs. Claus told me Shelly and Natalie had worked at Santa's Station for years.

"Honestly, I'd rather be shopping or hanging out with my friends." Shelly shrugged. "But my aunt and uncle needed someone with experience, and I couldn't let them down."

"Will we be working together every day?" I asked.

"Only if it's really busy," Shelly said. "I'm working extra today to train you. After this, you'll be on your own."

I was a little nervous as I fol-
lowed her out of the gingerbread house. I wanted to do
well so Mrs. Claus wouldn't be
sorry she hired me.

Mrs. Claus took the pictures
of kids sitting on Santa's lap.
She also ran the cash register.

If Mrs. Claus got backed up, Shelly helped get
photo orders ready for pick-up. She said that
putting pictures into the cardboard Santa Claus
frames was easy.

Keeping restless kids happy was the hard part.

"It won't take long to get the hang of it," Shelly
said. "Just open and close the rope gate and watch
what I do."

Shelly was right. The job seemed easy. The biggest
problems Shelly had were toddlers who were afraid
of Santa and parents who were short on time.

Half an hour later Shelly stepped back to let me
take over. "If you get a difficult customer, just keep
smiling and stay calm," she said. "You'll be fine."

"Got it." I nodded and took a deep breath. The
next child in line was a little girl. I opened the rope
gate and smiled. "Are you ready to see Santa?"

"Totally." She held up a long, long list.

The next kid was easy, too. After few more, I

relaxed and started to enjoy myself. Being a Santa Girl was fun! When Shelly wanted to take a Mocha-Freeze break, I was sure I could handle things. Besides, I had to go solo sooner or later.

The first little boy I sat on Santa's lap was a brat.

"Is this real?" The boy yanked on Santa's beard.

"Yes, it is. Ho, ho, ho." Santa gently pried the boy's fingers out of his beard, but he didn't get mad.

"Sorry, Santa," the boy's father apologized. "Tell Santa what you want, Jeff."

"I want my candy cane." Jeff pouted. "Right now."

Santa reached into the bag hanging on the throne, but it was empty. "Tell me what you want for Christmas, Jeff. Ashley will be right back with more candy canes."

"Coming right up!" I dashed over to the counter and asked Mrs. Claus for more candy canes.

"There should be several bags in there." Mrs. Claus pointed to a big plastic container under the counter.

I pulled out a new bag of candy canes and started back toward Santa. Suddenly a little girl started to cry. Then Jeff kicked Santa's leg.

"Jeffrey!" his father snapped. "That's enough! We're going home."

"No!" Jeff shrieked. "I want my candy cane!"

Another child in line started crying.

I didn't know what to do first! Then Santa frantically waved me over.

I ripped open the bag as I raced toward him. Candy canes went flying everywhere!

Jeff leaped off Santa's lap and grabbed two candy canes off the floor. Then he jumped off the platform. His father ran after him.

Santa slumped and sighed.

I dropped to my knees to gather up the plastic-wrapped candy canes.

"Ashley!" Mrs. Claus yelled. "You'll get your white tights dirty!"

I totally panicked and scrambled to my feet.

Two older kids jumped onto the platform, scooped up the candy canes, and bolted. The kids on line whined because they didn't have any, and three little kids started crying. Then a little girl spilled a large cup of soda. The sticky soda ran down the floor and over my green shoes.

Suddenly, I was positive I *couldn't* handle the job. I was the worst Santa Girl ever!

Chapter 6

Tuesday

Dear Diary,

I stood in the middle of Santa's
Station feeling sorry for myself for
three seconds. Then I remembered the
last thing Shelly had said to me: *Just keep smiling and
stay calm.*

I breathed slowly in and out. Since Jeff was
gone, I knew Santa didn't need candy canes right
away. So I handed out candy canes to all of the
kids waiting in line instead.

"Everyone gets a nice treat for being so patient,"
I said.

The kids were thrilled, and all the parents
thanked me. They had to wait while I picked up the
other scattered candy canes, but no one seemed to
mind.

The next boy wouldn't
stop crying when he sat on
Santa's lap. He didn't want a
candy cane, and he wouldn't
look at the camera. Not even
Santa could get him to smile.

"Oh, no! Not again!" I
cried. "How can this happen?" I suddenly slapped
my hand to my forehead.

41

Santa and the little boy both looked at me.

"What's the matter?" the boy's mother asked.

"I'm shrinking!" I slowly bent my knees so it looked like I was getting smaller. "Somebody laugh! Quick! Before I have to walk like a duck!"

The little boy giggled.

"Aha!" I stopped shrinking. "Better keep laughing until I get tall again!" By the time I straightened up, the little boy wanted to talk to Santa Claus.

The next little girl didn't want to give up her half-eaten candy cane. Santa didn't let kids with sticky candy sit on his lap. He didn't want to get anything stuck in his beard.

"I'll make you a deal, okay?" I squatted down so I was the same height as the girl. "I'll hold your candy cane while you talk to Santa. Then I'll give it back with two more!"

The little girl hesitated, but then she handed me her candy cane. "Don't eat it!"

"I won't." I held up my other hand. "Elf's honor."

I took a break when Shelly got back. Mrs. Claus stopped me as I ducked into the gingerbread house.

"I'm really impressed, Ashley," Mrs. Claus said, smiling. "I couldn't have picked a better Santa Girl."

Dear Diary,

Well, I've got good news and sort-of-good news today.

First the definitely good news: I have four people signed up to donate one dollar for every point I make in the charity basketball game!

The First Form teachers are dividing their support among the five players on the team. Mr. Gellar and Mrs. Quinones are backing me. I also signed up Mr. Harmon, who delivers groceries to the kitchen.

And you'll never guess who else! Not in a million years! Give up?

Jeremy Burke! Yes, my weird cousin, Jeremy. Do you believe it? I almost fell over!

"It's only a dollar a point, Jeremy." We were sitting on a bench outside Jeremy's dorm at the Harrington School for Boys.

"Yeah, but you'll probably make ten baskets, Mary-Kate," Jeremy said. "Two points a basket, that's twenty dollars!"

"But it's for a good cause," I pressed. "The money goes to the Toy Giveaway at the Community Center next week."

"Okay," Jeremy said.

"Really?" I frowned. My cousin loves to play pranks. "You're not just saying that so I'll go away, are you?"

Jeremy shook his head. "No, I mean it. I always get everything I want for Christmas. It will feel good to give something back."

Christmastime really is magical! Jeremy was the *last* person I expected to help out.

At lunch today, I told Ashley that Great-aunt Morgan was coming to visit and that Dana Woletsky had the vest.

"Dana?" Ashley gasped. "Now what are you going to do?"

"Ask Dana to give it back," I said.

"Good luck," Ashley said. "You'll need it."

The sort-of-good news is that after lunch I talked to Dana about Great-aunt Morgan's vest. Of course, she just *loved* the fact that she had something I wanted.

"I shouldn't have given my vest to Summer," I explained.

Dana and I sat in the Porter House lounge by the gorgeous tree. Evergreen garlands tied with red bows hung over every window and door.

I hoped the holiday atmosphere would make Dana feel like doing a good deed. After all, if *Jeremy* was willing to give money to charity, anything was possible!

"That's the ugliest vest I've ever seen," Dana said. "That's why I want to give it to my cousin Wanda as payback."

"Payback for what?" I asked, curious.

Dana grimaced. "Every Christmas she gives me something hideous, and every year my mother makes me wear it."

"Can't you buy Wanda something else?" I asked. "You might even find something that's more awful than my vest!"

"If it's so ugly, why do you want it back?" Dana asked.

I answered carefully. Dana has a habit of hurting people's feelings. If she met Great-aunt Morgan, she might accidentally or on purpose tell that I gave the vest away.

"It has sentimental value," I said.

Dana rolled her eyes. "I won't just give it to you."

"How much?" I was willing to pay to get the vest back. In a way, it would serve me right for re-gifting it to Summer.

"Not money," Dana said. "If you'll clean my room all day Saturday and do everything I say, you can have the vest."

"Do everything you say?" I cried. "No way!"

"Then no vest," Dana said with a smile. She knew I had no choice.

I took a deep breath. "I can't on Saturday," I explained. "I'm playing in the charity basketball game."

Dana frowned for a moment. "Okay, I'll wait until after the game, but then you're mine all day Sunday."

I hated the idea of being bossed around by Dana for a whole day. But it's my own fault. I wouldn't be in this mess if I hadn't given the vest to Summer in the first place.

Great-aunt Morgan's feelings were at stake. If a little humiliation was what it took, I was strong enough to handle it.

"Deal." I held out my hand, and we shook on it.

Dear Diary,

Today was payday. I've only been working at Santa's Station for three days, but I made thirty dollars! How cool is that?

I decided to buy the notebook for my dad first and save the rest of my money for a major shopping spree next week.

I felt very grown up as I walked through the mall. I always adore shopping, but spending money I earned feels better for some reason. The fact that I love my job is a bonus!

I stopped at Sports Mania to check on the skates.

"Are these skates still going on sale next Thursday?" I asked the saleswoman. She was the same one Summer and I talked to before.

"Yes, they are." She smiled. "What size was that?"

I told her and crossed my fingers as she checked for them on the store computer.

"Good news," the saleswoman said. "We've got several pairs in that size in stock."

"But there's still a whole week before the sale." I sighed. What if the skates sold out by then?

Then I had the best idea!

"Could I put the skates on layaway?" I asked. My grandma pays to have stores hold stuff all the time.

"Yes, but only at the regular price. If you put them on layaway today, you have to pay the whole forty dollars, not the sale price." The saleswoman shrugged. "Sorry."

I couldn't afford to pay forty dollars and get everything else on my list.

"That's okay," I said. "If there's really a Santa Claus, my sister's skates will still be here next week."

Don't laugh, Diary. I found a job that way, remember?

"For your sister, huh?" The woman nodded with a warm smile. "Well, Santa has never let me down before."

As I headed toward the luggage store, I just knew that everything was going to work out okay. I had a job, and the skates I wanted for Mary-Kate were going on sale.

But my amazing good luck was running out.

Last Sunday the luggage store had five small notebooks with plastic pages and three large ones. Today they were sold out of small notebooks. They only had two large notebooks left!

And the large notebook cost thirty-five dollars. That was ten dollars more than I planned to spend and five dollars more than I had!

"How much do I have to pay to hold this notebook for a week?" I asked the saleswoman.

"Ten dollars." The woman smiled when I handed her the notebook and my money.

I put the layaway slip in my wallet and left. I decided to make sure the other stores still had the gifts I wanted.

The bookstore had lots of movie-poster books. That was a relief! Especially because this morning I saw a Christmas package with my name on it from Phoebe. I didn't mean to snoop. It was sticking out from under Phoebe's bed. I pushed it back under

the bed and pretended I
hadn't seen it.

Phoebe's movie-poster
book wasn't a problem, but
the hobby store only had
three deluxe sets of History
Trivia Cards left on the
shelf. I couldn't take the chance. I put Ross's cards
on layaway for ten dollars. Then I dashed down the
mall to the Bed & Bath store.

I couldn't believe my eyes when I reached the
display of electric throw blankets. It was empty! I
ran over to a saleswoman. "Are you sold out of electric throw blankets?" I asked.

"I'm afraid so," she said.

"I saw one on the shelf by the sheets," a customer
behind me said. "Right over there."

"Thanks!" I ran in the direction the woman
pointed. She was right. There was one red-and-
green-plaid electric throw blanket on the shelf.
What luck!

I took the blanket to the checkout counter and
put it on layaway for ten dollars.

I left the store and sat on a bench to catch my
breath. At least my gifts for Great-aunt Morgan,
Ross, and Dad were safely on layaway. I pulled out
my list to update it.

Two of a Kind Diaries

WHO	GIFT	PRICE	$ OWED
Dad	Notebook	$35 ($10 layaway)	$25
M-K	Skates (on sale)		$30
Phoebe	Movie book		$15
Ross	History cards	$25 ($10 layaway)	$15
Aunt Morgan	Blanket	$30 ($10 layaway)	$20

Paid: $30   **Total owed** $105

MONEY TO SPEND: Dad's $25 + next week's pay $70 = $95

I stared at the numbers. I was ten dollars short!

I was so worried about getting the perfect gifts for Ross and Great-aunt Morgan, I forgot Dad's large notebook cost ten dollars more! Now the notebook, the trivia cards, and the blanket were on layaway. That meant I *had* to pay for them.

Worse, that meant I wasn't going to have enough money for Phoebe's book and Mary-Kate's skates!

Chapter 7

Friday

Dear Diary,

I needed ten more dollars. I wished I could split Great-aunt Morgan's gift with Mary-Kate, but she had already bought her something. Now I only had two choices: make more money or spend less.

Spending less meant giving Phoebe a different book, one she wouldn't like as much—or not getting Mary-Kate her skates. I couldn't do either one.

But I didn't know what to do. I already had a job. How could I make more money?

I wasn't in a very good mood when I went to work today. I tried not to let it show. Santa Girls can't be grumpy!

Just before my shift ended, Mrs. Claus went into the gingerbread house for a break. No one was waiting on line, and Santa dozed on the throne. I stood by the counter, guarding the locked cash register.

Shelly paused by the counter. She was wearing a beautiful green vest with a gold scroll design. "You look worried," she said. "Is something wrong, Ashley?"

"I had my whole gift list figured out to the last penny," I explained. "Then my dad's waterproof notebook turned out to cost ten dollars more than I

51

had planned for. Now I don't know what to do."

"Bummer," Shelly said. "So you need more money?"

I nodded. "But between school and working here, I can't get another job."

"Well, I was going to ask you for a favor," Shelly said. "But maybe we'll be doing each other one."

"What?"

"I really want to check out a couple of sales that end today," Shelly explained. "So if I leave two hours early and you fill in for me, you'll earn an extra ten dollars."

"That's *exactly* what I need!"

Two hours later I had enough to pay for Dad's large notebook. I felt so good, I hummed Christmas songs all the way back to Porter House. I sang "Deck the Halls" going up the stairs to my room, but the "fa la la la la" died in my throat when I read the note on my door.

ASHLEY BURKE OWES A $5.00 LIBRARY FINE FOR OVERDUE BOOKS. PLEASE PAY BEFORE CHRISTMAS VACATION BEGINS.

MRS. YANCOSEK

Oh, no! My stomach knotted as I opened the door. *How could I forget all about my library books?*

And how was I going to pay the fine? I'd just earned the extra ten dollars I needed for Dad's gift. Where was I going to get *another* five dollars? Every time I thought my money problem was solved, I wound up needing more money!

I was feeling pretty low when I went to dinner, but I tried to hide it. Everyone else seemed happy.

"Amazing news," Cheryl said. "I actually sang all my parts perfectly at rehearsal today. I wasn't nervous at all."

"So practicing with Mary-Kate helped?" Elise asked.

Cheryl grinned. "Boy, did it!"

"Sorry, I'm late." Mary-Kate pulled out a chair and sat down. "I was helping Robin practice foul shots."

"That's right!" Elise exclaimed. "The big charity basketball game is tomorrow."

I knew the charity basketball game was important to Mary-Kate, but I couldn't stop thinking about money. I stirred my pudding and frowned. Five dollars for a library fine wasn't much—except that I needed every penny I had for presents!

I wasn't really listening to the talk at our table. Someone must have said something about our chance to win.

Suddenly Summer yelled, "Go, White Oak!"

She totally startled me—just as I started to put a spoonful of chocolate pudding in my mouth!

I jumped.

And my spoon jerked.

The gob of pudding dropped off—right into Elise's lap!

"My new suede Christmas skirt!" Elise wailed. She jumped up. The pudding fell on the floor, but it left a big brown spot on the red skirt.

"I'm sorry!" I gasped.

"What am I going to do?" Elise cried. "My mom expects me to wear this skirt for Christmas when I go home!"

I stared at the brown spot. If I hadn't been day-dreaming, this wouldn't have happened!

Elise blotted the spot with a paper napkin, but that didn't help. "It's stained!"

"Don't panic," Mary-Kate said. "We don't go home for another week."

"You can have the skirt dry-cleaned," Cheryl said.

"Will dry-cleaning take the spot out?" Elise asked.

"I'm sure it will," I said. At least, I hoped so. I swallowed hard. "And I'll pay for it."

I couldn't afford ten dollars for dry-cleaning, but the stain on Elise's new skirt was my fault. Now I was short *fifteen* dollars for Christmas presents!

"Speaking of the charity basketball game—" Mary-Kate looked at me. "Will you pledge a dollar for every point I make tomorrow, Ashley?"

I nodded, but I felt sick. I couldn't refuse to support Mary-Kate in the charity basketball game. But now I had so many extra expenses, I wouldn't have any money left for presents!

Dear Diary,

I'm always a little nervous before a big game, and today was no different. I sat on the warm-up bench, watching the stands. The gym was packed with spectators for the charity game

All my friends were there to cheer the team, even

Jeremy and several other boys from Harrington. Ashley had to work.

"Okay, girls!" Coach clapped to get our attention. "Go out there and win one for Santa! White Oak is counting on you."

I stopped being nervous the instant I hit the court. Playing for charity is fun because it doesn't matter which team wins. But the White Oak team was hot. When the final buzzer sounded, our team was ahead by four points.

Summer high-fived everyone as we ran off the court. "You made nine baskets, Mary-Kate! How much money is that for the Toy Giveaway?"

I grabbed a towel off the bench and did the math in my head. Two points per basket was eighteen points. Everyone who supported me owed eighteen dollars. Eighteen times five was——

"Ninety dollars!" I said out loud.

"Wow!" Summer looked up and counted on her fingers. "I only made five baskets, but that's still sixty dollars!"

"And I made seventy," Lexy said.

I saw Dana walking toward me with Kristen Lindquist and Brooke Miller. I had been so into the game, I forgot all about my deal with Dana to get Great-aunt Morgan's vest back.

There was no point trying to avoid Dana and her friends. Tomorrow everyone would know what I'd agreed to do, anyway.

Dana and her friends edged into the group.

"Good game," Dana said.

"And it's good for those little kids who need free toys that you guys *like* doing sweaty stuff for fun," Kristen added.

I wondered if Kristen knew how horrible she sounded. If she did, she probably didn't care. Sometimes I think Kristen *tries* to be meaner than Dana!

Brooke's bag slipped off her shoulder and hit the floor with a *thud*.

"Oops." Brooke looked straight at me and smiled.

I just smiled back. Brooke was wearing a sweater, a pleated miniskirt, and suede shoes just like Dana. Brooke copied everything Dana did.

"Pick up that bag, Mary-Kate," Dana ordered.

"Hey!" Campbell frowned. "Since when does Mary-Kate take orders from you, Dana?"

"Since the game ended," Dana said. "Right, Mary-Kate?"

"Right." I picked up the bag and handed it to Brooke.

Summer, Campbell, and Lexy just stared at me.

It's going to be a long weekend, I thought with a sigh. From now until lights-out tomorrow night, Dana was the boss.

Chapter 8

Sunday

Dear Diary,

I went to Dana's room right after
breakfast. The oatmeal I ate for breakfast sat in my stomach like a heavy
rock. I knew Dana wouldn't make this easy on me,
and I was nervous.

When Dana opened the door, she didn't even say
hello!

"Well, I'm here," I stammered to fill in the awk-
ward silence. "Where do you want me to start—"

Dana cut me off. "I've made a list of things I want
you to do today, Mary-Kate. You don't have time to
waste talking."

My cheeks burned, but I couldn't complain.
Dana had Great-aunt Morgan's vest, and I had to
get it back.

Still, Diary, there's no way to
tell you how awful it was being
Dana's servant. Not in a few
sentences, anyway. So instead
I'll write down some of the
things she made me do.

"Closet first," Dana said as
she opened the closet door.

I ducked as several shoeboxes fell off the shelf. The whole closet was a mess of clothes, boxes, and other junk.

Dana handed me a black marker. "Mark all my shoeboxes so I know what's inside. Then put them back on the shelf."

I took the marker and went to work without a word.

Dana sat on her bed doing her nails. The only time she looked up was to say, "Faster, Mary-Kate. You're wasting time."

When I finished organizing Dana's shoes, she had me re-arrange her clothes—you won't believe it, Diary—according to season!

"Spring and fall on the left," Dana said. "Winter outfits in the middle, and summer on the right."

"What about stuff that isn't for a particular season?" I asked. "Things you can wear anytime."

Dana shrugged. "Put them between winter and summer."

It took almost two hours to switch the clothes around. I could have finished sooner, but I had to get Dana's nail polish from the dresser and hand her tissues from the desk. Then she asked me to fan her fresh polish until it was dry!

"Just blow on your polish, Dana," I snapped. "It will dry faster that way."

"You can't argue, Mary-Kate!" Dana snapped back. "Do you want your vest or not?"

I rolled my eyes and folded a piece of notebook paper to use as a fan.

I looked around for Great-aunt Morgan's vest, but it wasn't in the closet.

"What's next?" I asked.

Dana stood in front of the closet with her arms folded. "You know, I thought I wanted my clothes arranged this way, but now everything just looks all jumbled up."

I thought it was a good system, but it wasn't my closet.

"Arrange everything by color instead," Dana said.

"But I just finished doing it by season!" I exclaimed.

"Do it again," Dana said. "By color."

I shook my head in disgust, but I had to do whatever Dana said—all day.

After I finished the closet the second time, Dana had me alphabetize her CDs, first by artist and then by title.

Dana frowned at the CD rack when I stepped back. "We should do the CDs by

60

color, too. I want the CD cases to match the closet."

She had to be kidding. "In rainbow order?" I joked.

But I redid the CDs and polished all her boots and ironed all her blouses. I even sharpened all her pencils.

By the time I was finished, I was counting down the minutes until I could leave. Dana had gone to lunch and dinner without me. Luckily, she brought me back sandwiches.

I was glad that Dana wanted to watch a Christmas movie on TV that evening. At least I could sit down. Dana couldn't possibly think up enough errands to keep me running for the whole film!

Wrong!

"Go upstairs and get my blue sweater," Dana said.

I ran upstairs and got her blue sweater. Of course, she changed her mind when I gave it to her. She wanted the red sweatshirt. I ran upstairs again.

"I want a soda," Dana said during a commercial break.

I delivered her a soda. Then she wanted potato chips. Next it was gum.

I sagged with relief when the movie ended. It was ten minutes before bedtime. My day as Dana's servant was over!

Except for one final detail.

"I'll follow you up to your room to get my vest, Dana," I said. "Then you won't have to come all the way back down."

"You won't make it back to Porter House before lights-out," Dana said. "Just come back tomorrow to get it."

"I'll risk being late," I said. "I want my vest."

"No, you might get locked out," Dana argued. "You don't want to get in any more trouble, do you, Mary-Kate? Come back tomorrow." She turned and ran upstairs.

Dana had a point. I didn't want to get caught outside past curfew. Still, I had a bad feeling in the pit of my stomach as I ran all the way back to Porter House.

Dana wouldn't go back on a deal, would she?

Dear Diary,

Shelly's shift and mine overlapped today. Santa needs two helpers on busy weekend afternoons.

Right away, Shelly noticed my low mood.

"Now what's wrong?" she asked. "You've been

bummed out for two days. A sad Santa Girl isn't good for business."

"I know," I said.

"Want to talk about it?"

I didn't think there was any way to solve my money problem, but talking to Shelly might make me feel better. I certainly didn't want to get fired for not being jolly!

"Stuff keeps happening that costs me money I need for Christmas presents," I explained.

"On top of that ten dollars for your dad's gift?" Shelly asked.

I nodded. "I got a fine for overdue library books and a dry-cleaning bill. And I pledged money for my sister's charity basketball game. She made nine baskets."

"The same sister who wants ice skates?" Shelly asked. When I nodded, she added, "Well, I have an idea."

I held my breath.

"This is my fifth year as a Santa Girl, and it's just not as much fun as it used to be," Shelly said. "I'm just doing it to help my aunt and uncle, not because I need the money."

"Uh-huh." I didn't know what Shelly was trying to say.

Shelly continued. "So if it's okay with my aunt

and uncle, you can work more of my hours. Then I'll have some free time, and you'll make the money for your sister's skates."

I hugged Shelly. Santa Claus hadn't come to my rescue this time, but Shelly was just as good!

Now, if only our Santa and Mrs. Claus would agree.

"Absolutely not," Mrs. Claus said.

"No." Santa shook his head.

"Come on, Aunt Helen and Uncle Ralph," Shelly pleaded.

"I know you want to help Ashley," Mrs. Claus said, "but we can't let Ashley work extra hours. She's too young."

I felt awful as I left the mall and headed back to White Oak. Working extra hours at Santa's Station was my only chance to make more money.

When I got back to Porter House, I flopped on my bed and pulled out my list.

Santa Girls

WHO	GIFT	PRICE	$ OWED
Dad	Notebook	$35 ($10 layaway)	$25
M-K	Skates (on sale)		$30
Phoebe	Movie book		$15
Ross	History cards	$25 ($10 layaway)	$15
Aunt Morgan	Blanket	$30 ($10 layaway)	$20

Paid: $30 *Total owed* = $105

MONEY TO SPEND: Dad's $25 + next week's pay $70 = $95

+ Shelly's hours $10 = $105 (yea!)

NEW EXPENSES

Library fine	$5
Dry-cleaning	$10
M-K's baskets	$18

Total owed now: $138

$ I have: $105

$33 short!

I was so frustrated. I closed my eyes and muttered, "Help."

I just hoped the real Santa Claus was listening.

Chapter 9

Monday

Dear Diary,

People should listen to themselves. We get those funny feelings for a reason—because most of the time they're right!

After classes I ran to Phipps House to meet Dana.

"Oh, right," Dana said. "You want your vest."

"That was the deal," I said.

"Do you want to sell it?" she asked. "I *really* want to give it to Wanda. She'll just die when she has to wear it for Christmas dinner!"

"Sorry," I said. "I have to get it back. Now."

Dana opened her closet and began moving the hangers.

And I knew that something was seriously wrong. I had rearranged her closet *twice* yesterday. The vest wasn't there!

It wasn't there today, either.

I tried not to panic. "Where did you see it last?"

Dana paused then snapped her fingers. "The dining hall when Summer gave it to me! I remember putting the box on the chair beside me. I must have walked off without it."

I felt myself turn pale. "But, Dana—that was a week ago!"

Dana shrugged. "I've been so busy—"

I didn't wait to hear the rest of her excuses. I ran out the door and down the stairs. Maybe, just maybe, someone had found the vest and turned it in to the Lost and Found.

"There's nothing like that here, Mary-Kate," Mrs. Weinstock, the dining hall lady, told me a few minutes later.

"Are you sure?" I asked. I described it again. Mrs. Weinstock shook her head. "I don't remember seeing it, and I wouldn't forget a vest that looked like that."

"Thanks, anyway." I had a horrible feeling the vest had been thrown away. It was so ugly, nobody would want it!

I didn't know what to do next. There wasn't anything I *could* do—except turn to Ashley. She would understand.

"Dana lost the vest?" Ashley looked stunned.

"She said she left it in the dining hall, but it's not in the Lost and Found," I explained. "It's just gone!"

"Dana knew she didn't have it when she asked you to be her servant," Ashley fumed. "How could anyone be so mean?"

How could I be so trusting? I wondered.

But that wasn't what bothered me most.

"I can't even go buy another one," I moaned. "Great-aunt Morgan didn't just make the vest. She designed it, too. It's the only one like it in the whole universe!"

And I didn't have it to wear to lunch on Friday.

Dear Diary,

Poor Mary-Kate! She's so worried about having to tell Great-aunt Morgan her vest is gone. I couldn't stop thinking about her problem, but I didn't see any way out.

Shelly knew something was bothering me the minute I got to work. "Another problem or the same one?" she asked.

"Another one," I answered.

"I'm listening," Shelly said.

"It's my sister, Mary-Kate," I explained. "Our Great-aunt Morgan gave her a totally ugly vest for Christmas."

Shelly nodded. "And now Mary-Kate has to wear it?"

"She can't," I said. "Mary-Kate re-gifted the vest to someone else, who gave it to someone else. . . . "

Shelly looked puzzled. "Mary-Kate doesn't have it?"

"Nobody has it!" I threw up my hands. "It got lost or thrown away or something."

Shelly still looked confused. "If this vest is so awful, why does your sister want it back?"

"Because Great-aunt Morgan is taking us to lunch on Friday," I said. "If Mary-Kate doesn't wear the vest, our aunt's feelings will be hurt. Especially since Great-aunt Morgan knitted the vest from her own pattern."

"Knitted?" Shelly asked. "If you can draw a good picture of the vest, I can make another one. I love to knit."

It took a few seconds for Shelly's words to sink in.

"Seriously," Shelly said. "I make all my sweaters and caps. You've seen them."

"The green vest with the gold scroll design, too?"

Shelly nodded, and I started to get excited.

"I have a photograph of Mary-Kate in the vest!"

"No problem, then." Shelly grinned, then frowned. "Except one—actually, two."

"What?" I asked, worried.

"Friday is four days away," Shelly said. "That's not enough time to work here and make the vest, too. And Santa won't let you work any more hours."

There had to be a solution. Lots of people could be Santa Girls. But Shelly was the *only* person who could knit an emergency vest!

"Mary-Kate can work!" I cried. If Mary-Kate wanted the vest enough to be Dana's servant, she wouldn't mind being a Santa Girl so Shelly could make a new one.

"Okay," Shelly said. "And someone has to fill in for me at the Toy Giveaway tomorrow evening at the Community Center."

"I can do that!" I said. "Mary-Kate can work the evening shift here while I give away toys at the Community Center."

Shelly gave me a thumbs-up. "Then we've got a plan!"

Yeah, I thought. *And this is one plan that has to work!*

Chapter 10

Tuesday

Dear Diary,

"Are you sure Shelly can do it?" I asked Ashley. It was hard to believe anyone could really copy Great-aunt Morgan's vest.

"Positive," Ashley said. "I've seen the sweaters Shelly makes. I'll give her the photo of the vest to use as a guide."

"That's great!" I grinned from ear to ear.

"You can pay her for the supplies on Friday," Ashley said. "With your Santa Girl money."

"Right," I said. I was thrilled that I wouldn't have to disappoint Great-aunt Morgan. But I was not going to like being a Santa Girl. "Do I really have to wear that frilly Christmas elf outfit?" I asked.

Ashley rolled her eyes. "If I look adorable wearing it, so will you!"

I winced. "Looking adorable is not my style."

"Don't worry, Mary-Kate," Ashley assured me. "It's an easy, fun job! Most of the kids are on their best behavior because Santa is watching. I've only been kicked once."

Great, I thought. I've never been comfortable around little kids. But I didn't have a choice.

If I wanted a new vest, I had to work Shelly's hours at Santa's Station. Santa Girl, here I come.

Dear Diary,

Helping out at the Toy Giveaway made me feel fantastic. Probably because I was volunteering.

"Where's Shelly?" Captain John, the fire station chief, asked when I introduced myself.

"Something unexpected came up," I said.

The fire chief stared down at me with a doubtful frown.

Shelly's red Santa hat and red vest were huge on me. Captain John obviously thought I was just a kid who couldn't handle the job.

"I work with Shelly at the Santa's Station," I explained. "I'm an experienced elf."

"I'm sure you are." Captain John smiled. "Okay, we'll get started in a few minutes."

The Ladies Community Club had set up a table with punch and cookies. Half the people in the big hall were lined up for the snacks. The rest were

looking at the children's macaroni wreaths and Christmas pictures tacked to the walls.

Green and red paper chains hung from the ceiling. Strings of colored lights twinkled around the doors. Christmas music blared from a portable CD player.

"Ho, ho, ho!" Captain John stood on the stage holding a cordless microphone. "It's Christmas-present time!"

"Yeah!" the kids in the crowd cheered.

Captain John waved to me. I jumped onto the stage.

"We've got a new elf," Captain John said. "Ashley!"

The crowd applauded and I bowed.

"All right! Let's get started!" Captain John leaned over to whisper in my ear. "Just give the presents to the firefighters. They'll pass them out."

"Okay," I said. There were two piles of presents. I decided to stand between the piles.

Captain John turned up the music as I began handing out the gifts. Everyone was laughing and talking, and I wasn't the only one humming along to "Jingle Bells"!

Then the music suddenly stopped.

And silence settled over the big room.

Captain John checked the CD player. After a minute it was clear that the machine wasn't going to work.

"Sorry about that, folks," Captain John said with

a shrug. "We can't fix this broken boombox tonight."

I handed another present to a tall fireman. But now no one was talking or laughing or humming. The hall was filled with an awful quiet. Without music, the Christmas party just didn't feel like a party!

But, I realized, *that can be fixed!*

Before I could change my mind, I burst into song, just like they do in the movies.

"Dashing through the snow . . ." I sang as loudly as I could. I had no idea if my warbling, off-key voice was going to help, but I had to do something!

"In a one-horse open sleigh—" I waved my arms just like Ms. O'Neal did when she was directing the chorus. "Everybody sing! O'er the fields we go . . ."

By the end of the first verse, everyone in the hall was singing along! Even Captain John and the fire-fighters!

We sang and handed out presents for an hour. When we finished, everyone whistled and cheered.

"Let's give Ashley a big round of applause for a job well done!" Captain John grinned, and the crowd clapped wildly.

I didn't need any more thanks than that, but when the party ended some of the grown-ups started to tip me!

"That was good thinking, Ashley," one man said. He gave me five dollars and a pat on the back.

Getting tips was a total surprise. Back in my room, I counted them. I had twenty-two dollars in tips! I pulled out my list and added it in.

Total owed now: $138

$ I have: $105

$33 short
_____

$22 tips

still $11 short!
_____

Argh! I still don't have enough money!

Dear Diary,

I got to Santa's Station half an hour before Ashley's shift ended so she could show me what to do. Santa and Mrs. Claus had agreed to let me take Shelly's place. Even Mrs. Pritchard said it was okay. Shelly stopped by to pick up the photo of the vest.

"This means so much to me, Shelly," I said. "I don't know how to thank you."

"I'm happy to help," Shelly said. "I just hope I can find the same buttons and trim."

"Yeah," Ashley said. "I don't think a lot of people want green and yellow pom-pom trim."

"Probably not." Shelly put the picture in her bag. "Going to the yarn stores will take time, so I'd better get started."

I watched her go with a sinking feeling in my stomach. What if Shelly *couldn't* find the same buttons and trim?

"And you've got to start being a Santa Girl," Ashley said.

I learned by watching Ashley.

Ashley walked the kids up to Santa and lifted the smaller ones onto his lap. A few had to be convinced that Santa was a nice man. Bribing them with candy canes seemed to help.

I changed into the elf suit. It looked ridiculous. But I thought about how happy Great-aunt Morgan would be to see me in the new vest. Besides, it wasn't nearly as bad as being Dana's servant.

"It's only for three days," I muttered as I stepped out of the gingerbread house.

"You'll do fine, Mary-Kate," Mrs. Claus said.

I walked up to the rope gate. Ashley stayed to help for a few minutes, but after the first few kids, I knew the routine.

Ashley took off for the Toy Giveaway, and I was on my own. Taking a deep breath, I unhooked the rope gate to let the next boy and his mother through. "I guess you're next," I said.

"Yahoo!" The boy charged past me.

His mother and I were *both* caught off guard.

I ran after him, but the kid barreled into Santa before I caught up. The little guy leaned against Santa's knees and launched into his Christmas wish list.

"I want a superset of building blocks, and a remote-controlled car, and an extra battery for it, five electronic games, and a soccer ball, and a DVD player for my room."

When the boy paused to take a breath, I grabbed his hand. "Sorry, Santa. He surprised me."

"They do that sometimes," Santa said, smiling.

Whew! Santa didn't blame me!

The boy's mother didn't want a picture. Santa gave him a candy cane, and I went back to get the next kid.

The little girl at the head of the line looked scared. I gave her a smile. "I bet you can't wait to see Santa, huh?"

She sniffled for a second, then suddenly started to shriek. Her mother picked her up and tried to quiet her.

"Uh—I didn't mean to scare her," I stuttered.

"It's not your fault," the girl's mother said. "Amy

is always shy around people she doesn't know."

"No Santa! No Santa!" Amy screeched.

Ashley would have known how to handle this, but I didn't have a clue. I just watched helplessly as the woman left with her sobbing daughter.

Suddenly, I saw Mrs. Claus watching me. I couldn't tell if she was angry, but I knew I had to do better.

Of course, whenever you think that, things get worse.

A horrid little boy pulled my hat off my head. Another little girl slid off Santa's knee every time I lifted her up. Her mom was holding a baby and couldn't help.

Then a woman asked for several photos of her little girl. She wanted a perfect picture and was willing to pay for as many shots as it took. Santa and Mrs. Claus wanted people to be happy with their photos, so they couldn't refuse, but it was hard on the other customers.

"How much longer is this going to be?" an irritated father demanded. "Bradley has been waiting for thirty minutes."

"Yeah!" Bradley jutted out his chin and scowled.

They had only been waiting for twenty minutes, but I didn't argue. I just tried to calm down the father. "It won't be much longer, sir," I said.

"Oh, yes!" said the mother who was getting the pictures. "Hold that pose, darling! That's perfect."

Thank goodness, I thought.

In that split second, when I wasn't paying attention, Bradley ducked under the rope.

This time I was caught off guard and off balance. As Bradley ran by me toward Santa, I stumbled backward. I backed right into a plastic reindeer. It started to fall over.

Bradley charged across the platform, yelling, "My turn! I'm next!"

I gasped. Bradley was about to ruin the fussy mother's perfect picture.

"No! Stop!" The mother waved frantically at Bradley.

The reindeer was falling over behind me. It was going to hit two giant candy canes and a Christmas tree! If the Christmas tree fell over, it would crash into the sleigh full of presents. Santa's Station would be wrecked!

Two disasters were happening at the same time. And I could only stop one of them!

Chapter 11

Tuesday

Dear Diary,

I made an instant decision.

If the picture was ruined, the fussy mom would keep asking for more shots. The line might be backed up to the Video Mart before she got another shot she liked! Still, a bad photo would be a lot easier to fix than a wrecked Santa's Station!

I sprang into action and grabbed the plastic antlers in both hands. The reindeer stopped falling just as it hit the giant candy canes.

The big candy canes wobbled. I stood the reindeer upright. Then I caught the candy canes before they smashed into the Christmas tree. I pushed the candy canes upright. I saw Mrs. Claus frown at me! Didn't she know I had just stopped half the Santa's Station decorations from toppling like dominoes?

Maybe not, I thought as her face darkened.

Santa, the kids and parents in line, and the woman who wanted a good picture were *all* staring at me!

Mrs. Claus walked over to me. "What just happened, Mary-Kate?" she asked.

"Well, that boy ran under the rope and I tripped

and the reindeer fell," I said. "But then I caught it."

Mrs. Claus was still frowning.

She thinks I tripped first! I realized. How could I prove that Bradley ducked under the rope and ran into me?

"Way to go, Santa Girl!" Campbell's voice broke through the stunned silence.

I looked around to see my roommate, Lexy, and Summer standing by the edge of the platform.

"We saw the *whole* thing," Summer said. "That little kid pushed Mary-Kate into the reindeer."

"That's right," Lexy agreed. "And if Mary-Kate hadn't moved fast, Santa's Station would be a disaster right now."

"Everything on the stage would be ruined," Summer said.

My friends knew it wasn't my fault! They wanted to make sure Santa and Mrs. Claus knew it, too.

"Well, that's what I thought I saw," Mrs. Claus admitted.

"Then you believe me?" I asked.

"Yes," Mrs. Claus said. "Now let's get back to work."

"Three cheers for the elf!" Campbell began to applaud. Then the people in line started clapping.

I stepped closer to my friends. "Thanks for sticking up for me."

"It's the least we could do," Campbell said. "You helped all of us when we needed it."

"Besides, we just told the truth," Summer added.

"Right." Lexy nodded. "That little boy was to blame."

Bradley's father hurried over to Santa. "I am so sorry. Bradley is a little overexcited about Christmas. I'll be more than happy to pay for the ruined photo."

"That won't be necessary," Santa said. "It's just too bad we missed that perfect shot."

"But we didn't." Mrs. Claus called the fussy mom over to look. "I got the picture before Bradley entered the frame."

"Fabulous!" The mom grinned. "I'll take two dozen picture ornaments and two dozen photos in Santa frames."

Mrs. Claus gave me a thumbs-up and smiled.

"Catch you later, Mary-Kate!" Campbell waved as she and my fantastic friends moved on.

After all the excitement, the people in line relaxed. That made my job easier. I actually started enjoying myself.

Until I glanced around the mall and saw Shelly coming out of Teen Town with her friends.

Upsetting questions began to flash through my mind. *Why isn't Shelly shopping for supplies? What if she can't find the buttons or the trim? What if she doesn't finish the vest by Friday noon?*

Dear Diary,

I can't believe this is the end of my career as a Santa Girl! Today was my last day on the job. It was Mary-Kate's last day, too. She isn't upset, but I'll miss it.

Santa and Mrs. Claus said they'd miss me, too!

"You've been a wonderful Santa Girl, Ashley," Mrs. Claus said. "I am so glad I gave you a chance."

Santa handed me my pay envelope and then gave me a second one.

"What's this?" I asked.

Santa grinned. "A little bonus for being a great helper."

It wasn't a little bonus. Santa gave me twenty-five dollars! I had the eleven dollars I needed to buy Phoebe's book and Mary-Kate's skates, *plus* four-teen dollars left over!

I was so excited and grateful, I hugged both Santa and Mrs. Claus. Then I dashed through the mall to Sports Mania.

Sure enough, the Olympic Gold ice skates were on sale for thirty dollars. I ran to the display and began sorting through the boxes, looking every-

 where for Mary-Kate's size. I couldn't find any! I searched the boxes again. And again.

I couldn't find any skates in Mary-Kate's size.

All my work and worry, and now no skates! That's all Mary-Kate wanted for Christmas. I had to get them for her!

Then I remembered that the saleswoman had used the computer to check the stock in the storeroom.

"Do you have more skates in the back?" I asked the young man behind the counter. The saleswoman wasn't there.

"Nope," he answered. "I put all our skates out on the display this morning."

"Are you sure?" My voice trembled. It wasn't fair. I had worked so hard to get Mary-Kate's skates.

The young man nodded. "Sorry."

I sank into a chair by the ski parkas and blinked back tears.

Santa had given me a bonus so I could have a Merry Christmas. But it wouldn't be a very Merry Christmas for me if I couldn't give Mary-Kate her Olympic Gold ice skates.

Chapter 12

Thursday

Dear Diary,

I'm not sure how long I sat there by the ski parkas. Finally I heard someone say, "Are you okay?"

It was the saleswoman I'd met before.

"Not really." My voice trembled. "All the skates in Mary-Kate's size are gone."

"Yes, I'm sorry. We have strict rules about holding merchandise," the saleswoman explained, "or I would have set aside a pair of skates for you."

"That's okay," I said. "I wouldn't want you to get into trouble for me."

"Oh, I won't get in trouble." She smiled and walked behind the counter.

What does that mean? I wondered as the saleswoman ducked down. I swallowed hard when she stood up and set a skate box on the counter.

"Luckily, we don't have *any* rules about putting returned merchandise back on the shelves," she said. "These were exchanged for another size on Tuesday."

"They were?" I asked, standing up.

The saleswoman nodded and turned the box so I could read the label on the end. "This is your sister's size, right?"

"Yes!" I inhaled sharply. The box had Olympic Gold skates in Mary-Kate's size! "You saved these for me?"

The saleswoman shrugged. "Santa asked me for a favor. I couldn't say no. It's Christmas!"

She was teasing me, but I didn't mind.

"Thank you!" I said. I paid for the skates and rushed to the bookstore to get Phoebe's present.

Dear Diary,

I was too tired to wrap the book and skates when I got back to my room last night. Good thing, too, because Phoebe came in a minute after I did. She would have caught me in the act!

I wrapped the skates and the book while Phoebe was using the bathroom this morning.

"For me?" Phoebe asked when she came back and saw the present on her bed.

"I wanted you to have it before you go home tomorrow," I explained.

"I've got one for you, too." Phoebe pulled her gift out from under the bed. "Do you think we should wait until Christmas to open them?" she asked.

"No," I said, grinning. I never want to wait to open presents. Neither did Phoebe.

"Okay, I'll go first." Phoebe sat on her bed and ripped the paper. Her eyes got wide when she saw the title of the book. "Wow! A book of old movie posters! This is fantastic!"

"I guess you like it, huh?" I teased.

"Totally! Open yours," Phoebe said.

"Okay." I slipped the elastic ribbon off the corners of the box and lifted the lid. I pulled out a black leather shoulder bag that matched my new jacket exactly! "Oh, Phoebe! This is perfect!"

"I guess you like it, huh?" Phoebe asked.

"Totally!" To prove it, I switched everything out of my old bag into the new one.

I stayed behind when Phoebe left for lunch. I had to finish packing for Christmas break. Mary-Kate and Great-aunt Morgan would be arriving any minute.

Someone knocked on my door. I quickly put Mary-Kate's wrapped skates in my suitcase and closed it. I wanted to give Mary-Kate the skates right then and there! But I also wanted to surprise her on Christmas morning. I decided to wait.

"Has Shelly been here?" Mary-Kate sounded frantic.

"No." I frowned. Great-aunt Morgan would be

here soon. Shelly was cutting things pretty close. "Where did you tell Shelly to go?" I asked.

"I gave her both room numbers, but I didn't want to wait by myself." Mary-Kate perched on the edge of Phoebe's bed. Someone else knocked a moment later. We both froze.

Was it Shelly or Great-aunt Morgan?

Mary-Kate covered her eyes with her hands.

I opened the door. "Shelly! Are we glad to see you!"

Mary-Kate jumped up to check out the new vest. "I can't believe it!" she exclaimed.

We looked at the new black vest, then at the photo. The new vest was identical to the one Great-aunt Morgan had made. Even the green and yellow pom-pom trim matched.

"It's perfect!" Mary-Kate said.

"Almost," Shelly said. "The yellow buttons aren't exactly the same color."

"Well, I can't tell the difference," I said. I never doubted that Shelly could do the job, but I was still amazed.

Mary-Kate paid Shelly for the supplies and her time. I gave her a ten-dollar tip from my bonus.

Shelly didn't want to take it. "You have to," I said. "You totally earned it!"

Five seconds later there was another knock.

Great-aunt Morgan was here!

Dear Diary,

I've had some close calls in my life, but getting the vest from Shelly a whole minute before Great-aunt Morgan showed up was one of the closest!

I put on the vest on while Ashley squeezed Great-aunt Morgan in a hug.

"Oh, my!" Great-aunt Morgan laughed. "What a wonderful welcome!"

"Hi, Aunt Morgan." I gave her a kiss on the cheek. When I stood back, she noticed I was wearing the vest.

"It does fit you perfectly, doesn't it, dear?" Great-aunt Morgan beamed.

"Like it was made just for me," I said. *Twice!* I thought with a grin.

"Are you two hungry?" Great-aunt Morgan asked.

"Starved!" Ashley grabbed her red mittens and the new jacket.

It made me smile to see Ashley wear the jacket I had gotten her. That's how I knew Great-aunt Morgan would be crushed if I didn't have her vest.

Then Ashley picked up an awesome black leather shoulder bag.

"Is that bag new?" I asked. "It goes great with the jacket."

"Phoebe gave it to me for Christmas," Ashley said. "It's a perfect match."

We went downstairs. We stopped in the lounge to show Great-aunt Morgan the Christmas tree.

"My, what a wonderful tree," Great-aunt Morgan exclaimed. "I like candy canes and red bows on a tree."

"That was Elise's idea," Ashley said.

"Elise is one of our best friends," I said. I glanced toward the fireplace. Jolene Dupree was staring at me from across the room. And she was wearing my vest!

"How did Jolene get your vest?" Ashley asked.

"I don't know," I whispered back. "You keep Aunt Morgan busy and away from Jolene. I'm going to find out."

Ashley steered Great-aunt Morgan closer to the tree. I walked over to Jolene. She glared at me—as if I had just shown up in the vest *her* great-aunt had made!

"Where did you get that vest, Mary-Kate?" Jolene demanded.

"Someone made it for me," I said. I didn't understand why she was so angry, but I kept my cool. "Where did you get yours?"

"From Dana Woletsky!" Jolene looked very annoyed. "She told me it was a one-of-a-kind original. Dana wanted it for her cousin, but I gave her ten dollars."

"Ten dollars?" I was stunned. "When?"

"Last week," Jolene said. "Tuesday, I think."

So Dana didn't have my vest when she asked me to be her servant! I thought, fuming.

The funny thing was, so many people actually *wanted* Great-aunt Morgan's ugly vest! I had regifted it to Summer, who gave it to Dana, but Jolene had paid for it!

"Well, don't worry, Jolene," I said. "I can absolutely guarantee that there are only *two* vests like this in the whole world. And after today, I'll never wear mine again."

I was totally furious with Dana. Before I could think of what to do, Great-aunt Morgan came up behind me.

"Mary-Kate where did that girl get a vest like yours?" Great-aunt Morgan asked. "It's my own original design."

"Yes, and—" I cleared my throat, hoping for a burst of sudden brilliance.

Ashley jumped in. "Jolene liked Mary-Kate's vest so much, she had one made just like it."

That wasn't quite the honest truth, but we had to protect Great-aunt Morgan's feelings.

"Really?" Great-aunt Morgan's eyes lit up with pride. "Why, isn't that lovely. Maybe I should make more. . . ."

I changed the subject. "Let's go eat. I'm starved!"

Dear Diary,

Life can be strange sometimes, but I guess all's well that ends well. Great-aunt Morgan will never know that Mary-Kate re-gifted the ugly black vest. Mary-Kate shouldn't have given the handmade vest away, but she worked hard to make things right.

Dana was the only loose end in the whole mess. Mary-Kate and I discussed it in her room after lunch.

"I can't let Dana get away with this." Mary-Kate sat propped against her pillows with her arms folded.

I sat at the end of the bed. I didn't blame my sister for being furious. Dana had sold the vest to Jolene *before* she told Mary-Kate she could work to get it back.

"It's not really in the spirit of Christmas to want revenge," I said, "even if Dana does deserve it."

"Yeah, I know." Mary-Kate sighed. "Since it's Christmas, I'm going to let this one go." Then she smiled. "But there's always next year!'

"Spoken like a true Santa Girl," I teased. She was being such a good sport, I decided to do something nice for her. I pulled the wrapped skates out of my suitcase.

"It's not Christmas yet." Mary-Kate's eyes shone with excitement.

"Well, you gave me my jacket early, so it doesn't seem fair to make you wait." I handed her the box. I couldn't wait to see her face when she opened the package.

"Skates!" Mary-Kate's eyes got wider when she opened the box. "Olympic Gold skates! *Exactly* what I wanted!"

"Does that mean you like them?" I asked.

"Yes!" Mary-Kate leaned forward to hug me. "But to be honest, I'm not sure which is better: my skates, or knowing how hard you worked at Santa's Station to get them."

"Except that I loved being a Santa Girl," I said. "I had so much fun, it didn't seem like working at all."

"I'm glad you liked it!" Mary-Kate wrinkled her nose. "I will *never* re-gift anything ever again. My Santa Girl days are over!"

We both laughed.

Mary-Kate had her skates, and giving them to her made me feel great. Maybe that's why Santa Claus had so many helpers this year! Giving really *is* more fun than getting.

It looked like it was going to be a very Merry Christmas after all.

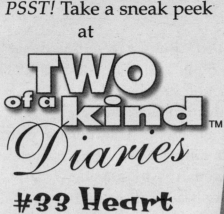

MARY-KATE'S DIARY

Dear Diary,

I had every reason to believe that this was going to be a super day. For starters, our Heart-O-Gram business was already booming. By late afternoon I had sung five Heart-O-Grams on campus. I was totally psyched!

"Did we raise enough money for a DVD player yet?" Cheryl asked back at the Acorn office.

"We only raised enough money for a third of a DVD

player," Phoebe replied. "But we're getting there!"

Cheryl, Phoebe, Elise, and I dug through the Heart-O-Gram basket on Phoebe's desk. We pulled out a few and read them to ourselves.

"Uh-oh," Cheryl groaned. "This person wants me to sing a poem in Italian."

"And this girl wants me to sing her Heart-O-Gram standing on my head!" Elise cried.

I smiled as I unfolded a form. A five-dollar bill was stapled to the corner. Carefully I pulled off the bill and slipped it in the box next to the basket.

Okay, I thought, reading the form. *This Heart-O-Gram is for . . .* I blinked a few times as I read the boy's name over and over. Then I looked up at my friends and said, "You guys, this Heart-O-Gram is for Jordan Marshall—my boyfriend!"

"Who sent it?" Phoebe asked.

"I don't know," I said. "The Sent By section is blank."

Then I took a deep breath and read the Heart-O-Gram out loud: "'Dear Pookie . . .'"

"'Pookie'?" Cheryl said, wrinkling her nose.

"'You will always be the sunshine in my life. Stay as sweet as you are. From, You Know Who.'"

"'You Know Who,'" Elise said slowly. "Who is 'You Know Who'?"

That's what I wanted to know!

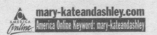

Mary-Kate
as Misty

Ashley
as Amber

Let's go
save the world...
again!

MARY-KATE AND ASHLEY
iN ACTION!
only on

TOON Disney
CHANNEL℠

**Call your cable operator
or satellite provider
to request Toon Disney.**

ToonDisney.com ©Disney

mary-kateandashley

GREAT
HAIRSTYLES
ARE AS
EASY AS...

1 CURL IT!

2 STRAIGHTEN IT!

3 CRIMP IT!

SO MANY LOOKS
TO CHOOSE FROM!

CURL & STYLE
Fashion Dolls

Dolls for Real Girls

With the new Mary-Kate and Ashley
Curl & Style fashion dolls, you can
create the same cool hairstyles
you see them wear in their
TV series' and movies!

So many looks to
choose from with hair
accessories and an
additional fashion!

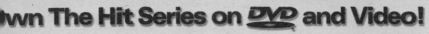